Wombat Goes Walkabout

Michael Morpurgo

Christian Birmingham

HarperCollins *Children's Books*

For Alice and Lucie
MM

To Penny and Cathy
CB

The illustrator would like to thank Jackie French, Healesville Sanctuary,
Jirrahlinga Koala and Wildlife Sanctuary, HarperCollins Australia and Birdworld

Also published by HarperCollins:

Sam's Duck by Michael Morpurgo & Keith Bowen

The Magical Bicycle by Berlie Doherty & Christian Birmingham
The Sea Of Tranquility by Mark Haddon & Christian Birmingham
Windhover by Alan Brown & Christian Birmingham

This edition published by HarperCollinsChildren's Books in 2012

First published in Picture Lions in 2000

First published in hardback in Great Britain
by HarperCollins Publishers Ltd in 1999

1

ISBN: 978-0-00-791412-8

Text copyright © Michael Morpurgo 1999
Illustrations copyright © Christian Birmingham 1999
The author and illustrator assert the moral right
to be identified as the author and illustrator of this work.

Visit our website at: www.harpercollins.co.uk
Printed and bound in the UK

One day Wombat woke up and thought, "I think I'll dig a hole today." Wombat loved digging holes. So off he went and dug a deep, deep hole. He crawled inside and sat there in the cool and the dark and began to think, because Wombat loved thinking too. He thought to himself, "Why is the sky blue? Why am I a wombat and not a kangaroo?"

Some time later, Wombat climbed out of his hole.

He looked around for his mother, but she wasn't there.

He was all alone.

"Who are you?" cried Kookaburra
from high in the sky.
"I'm Wombat," said Wombat.
"And what can you do, Wombat?"
"Not much. I dig a lot
and I think a lot."
"That's nothing," cackled Kookaburra.
"I can fly. Look at me."
And he looped the loop
and flew away.

Wombat went down to the creek
to look for his mother.
But she wasn't there either.
Just then Wallaby came hopping by.
"Who are you?" he asked, looking
down his nose at Wombat.
"I'm Wombat," said Wombat.
"And what can you do, Wombat?"
"Not much. I dig a lot
and I think a lot."
"That's nothing," laughed Wallaby.
"I can hop. I can skip. I can jump.
Look at me." And he hopped and
skipped and jumped away.

Wombat walked and walked,
and everywhere he walked he looked
for his mother. But he couldn't see her
anywhere. He sat down under a
stringy bark gum tree to get his
breath back. Just then Possum
popped up beside him.
"Who are you?" she asked, darting
her eyes this way and that.
"I'm Wombat," said Wombat.
"And what can you do?"
"Not much. I dig a lot
and I think a lot."
"That's nothing," laughed Possum.
"I can hang upside down.
I can swing by my tail. Look at me!"
And she swung away up the
stringy bark gum tree.

Wombat wandered sadly through the
bush, still looking for his mother.
Just then Emu came scampering by.
"Who are you?" he snapped.
"I'm Wombat," said Wombat.
"And what can you do?"
"Not much. I dig a lot
and I think a lot."
"That's nothing," laughed Emu.
"I can scamper. I can scoot
around in crazy circles. Look at me!"
And away he scampered, scooting
around in crazy circles.

Just then Boy came by,
hunting after Emu.
"Who are you?" he asked.
"I'm Wombat," said Wombat.
"And what can you do?"
"Not much. I dig a lot
and I think a lot."
"That's nothing," laughed Boy.
"I can do just about everything.
I can jump, I can run, I can swing.
I can even hunt. Look at me."
And off he went,
hunting after Emu.

It was baking hot now, and Wombat
shuffled into the shade of a great
eucalyptus tree. He hoped his mother
might be there. But she wasn't.
"Who are you?" called Koala from
way up in the tree above him.
"I'm Wombat," said Wombat.
"And what can you do?"
"Not much. I dig a lot
and I think a lot."
"That's nothing," laughed Koala.
"I can doze, I can snooze, I can snore.
Look at me." And very soon she was
dozing and snoozing and snoring away
high up in her eucalyptus tree.
By now Wombat was very, very tired.
So he lay down in the shade
and sang himself to sleep.

When Wombat woke up,
he looked around for his mother.
But she still wasn't there.
"I know," he thought. "I'll climb
the highest hill I can find.
Surely I'll be able to see her then."
So that's what he did.
He climbed and he climbed
and he climbed.

When he
reached the top
he looked about him.
Everywhere he looked there
were lots of cackling kookaburras,
hopping wallabies, swinging possums,
hunting boys, scampering emus, and
dozing koalas. But no matter how hard he
looked, he just couldn't see his mother anywhere.

But he did see something else.
He saw smoke. He saw fire.
It was leaping from tree to tree.
It was coming straight towards him.
Wombat thought hard, very hard.
Suddenly he knew what to do.
He ran down the hill as fast as
he could, and began to dig.
He dug and he dug and he dug.

Then Kookaburra came by, and Wallaby and Possum
and Emu and Boy and Koala. "Fire!" they all cried.
"Run, run, you silly Wombat. Fire! Fire!"
    But Wombat just went on digging.

"What are you doing?"
they asked.
    "I'm digging," replied Wombat.
"And I'm thinking too."
    "What are you thinking?" they cried.
    "I'm thinking that fire burns faster
than you can run or fly or hop or swing.
And I'm thinking that there's plenty of room
down in my hole if you want to join me.
We'll be quite safe."
    They took just one look at all the crackling fire and
all the billowing smoke. One look was all they needed.

Down into Wombat's hole they jumped, until they were
all sitting there, safe and snug. And to keep them all
happy Wombat sang them the digging song that his
mother had taught him.

When at last it was all over (the fire and the song) they climbed out into the evening air.

"I wish," sighed Wombat, looking around him sadly. "I just wish I could find my mother. I've lost her and she's lost me."

"Well, why didn't you ask?" they all said. "We'll find her for you." And away they went, flying and swinging, hopping and scampering, running around in all directions.

With so many of them looking, it wasn't
long before they found Wombat's mother,
and brought her back to him.

Wombat and his mother just hugged and
hugged and hugged.

"I've been looking everywhere for you," she cried.
"I was worried sick. What've you been up to?"

"Not much, Mum," Wombat said.
"I've just been thinking a lot,
and digging a lot.
That's all."